Welcome to ALADDIN QUIX!

If you are looking for fast, fun-to-read stories with colorful characters, lots of kid-friendly humor, easy-to-follow action, entertaining story lines, and lively illustrations, then **ALADDIN QUIX** is for you!

But wait, there's more!

If you're also looking for stories with tables of contents; word lists; about-the-book questions; 64, 80, or 96 pages; short chapters; short paragraphs; and large fonts, then **ALADDIN QUIX** is *definitely* for you!

ALADDIN QUIX: The next step between ready to reads and longer, more challenging chapter books, for readers five to eight years old.

Also by Joan Holub and Suzanne Williams

Goddess Girls series
Heroes in Training series
Thunder Girls series
Little Goddess Girls series

SCHOOL FOR MAGICAL MONSTERS
Rise of Pegasus

JOAN HOLUB & SUZANNE WILLIAMS
ILLUSTRATED BY TOBY ALLEN

ALADDIN QUIX
New York London Toronto Sydney New Delhi

For Heidi, Louise, Chuck, and Gene, my beloved
grandchildren
—S. W.

For kids like you who enjoy books
with excitement, magic, and laughs!
—J. H.

This book is a work of fiction. Any references to historical events, real people, or real places are used fictitiously. Other names, characters, places, and events are products of the author's imagination, and any resemblance to actual events or places or persons, living or dead, is entirely coincidental.

ALADDIN QUIX
Simon & Schuster Children's Publishing Division
1230 Avenue of the Americas, New York, New York 10020
First Aladdin QUIX hardcover edition July 2024
Text copyright © 2024 by Joan Holub and Suzanne Williams
Illustrations copyright © 2024 by Toby Allen
Also available in an Aladdin QUIX paperback edition.
All rights reserved, including the right of reproduction in whole or in part in any form.
ALADDIN and the related marks and colophon are trademarks of Simon & Schuster, LLC.
Simon & Schuster: Celebrating 100 Years of Publishing in 2024
For information about special discounts for bulk purchases, please contact Simon & Schuster Special Sales at 1-866-506-1949 or business@simonandschuster.com.
The Simon & Schuster Speakers Bureau can bring authors to your live event. For more information or to book an event contact the Simon & Schuster Speakers Bureau at 1-866-248-3049 or visit our website at www.simonspeakers.com.
Designed by Tiara Iandiorio
The illustrations for this book were rendered digitally.
The text of this book was set in Archer Medium.
Manufactured in the United States of America 0624 LAK
2 4 6 8 10 9 7 5 3 1
Library of Congress Control Number 2022058274
ISBN 9781665917711 (hc)
ISBN 9781665917704 (pbk)
ISBN 9781665917728 (ebook)

Cast of Characters

᚛᚛᚛ CREATURES ᚛᚛᚛

Cyclops (SI•clops): tall girl with only one eye

Griffin (GRIFF•en): half-eagle, half-lion boy

Hippocampus (hip•uh•KAMP•us): girl horse with a fish tail

Minotaur (MI•no•tohr): boy bull

Pegasus (PEG•uh•suss): boy horse

Sphinx (SFINGKS): girl with a human head, eagle wings, and a lion body

BEASTS

Cerberus (SER•burr•us): three-headed dog boy

Chimera (ky•MEER•uh): girl with a lion head, a goat head, and a dragon head

Geryon (JEE•ree•uhn): boy with three heads and bodies, four wings, and stinky breath

OTHERS

Mr. Chiron (KY•rawn): schoolteacher centaur (part man, part horse)

Zeus (ZOOSS): boy, king of the gods in Greek mythology

Contents

Chapter 1: Pegasus Trips Up — 1

Chapter 2: School for Magical Monsters — 10

Chapter 3: First Day of Class — 25

Chapter 4: *Zzzt!* — 36

Chapter 5: Beast Bash — 47

Chapter 6: Magic Wings — 63

Word List — 81

Questions — 83

Authors' Note — 85

Pegasus Trips Up

Hi, I'm **Pegasus**. I'm a horse, of course. And I'm a Creature, too—a **mythical** being. See this trail I'm climbing? It goes almost to the top of **Mount Olympus**. I've been invited to the **School for Magical**

Monsters up there. Tomorrow's my first day. It's gonna be great!

At my old school I didn't really fit in. I was the *only* Creature there. But I've heard that lots of Creatures go to my new school. I can't wait to meet them!

Flap! Flap! **Yikes!** A big pair of sparkly white wings swoops down from the sky. The wings aren't attached to anything. Not to a bird, a dragon, or a fairy!

Whoosh! Those wings zoom straight at me. Their feathers almost get **tangled** in my mane! I shake myself all over till they fly away.

Eek! They dive-bomb me again! I whirl. I twirl. But I'm a little **clumsy**. This time I stumble. I trip over a rock and land on my belly. **KERPLUNK!**

Okay, it's true. I'm a *lot* clumsy! But the wings fly skyward again. Guess I showed them. Ha!

"Hey, you! Fancy-dancy pants!" a voice booms. "I'm trying to catch those wings. Stop scaring them away!"

I leap up to see a boy with black hair. "Why do you want them?" I ask.

The boy rolls his eyes. "Duh? Because they have magic."

"Awesome!" I say. "I'm gonna get my own magic soon. I don't know what it'll be yet, but at my new school everyone finds a special power sooner or later. When I finally get mine I guess I could call it my . . . er . . . *horsepower*." I laugh at my silly joke. *Snort! Snort!*

"Lucky you," says the boy. "I could use some magic myself. *Wing* magic!"

"What for, though?" I ask.

The boy doesn't say. Instead, he looks me over. "Hey! You're a Creature, right?" he says. "That's cool."

Cool? I'm not used to

such respect. At my old school, I got *teased* for being different and clumsy. So I smile at him. "Mmm-hmm."

Flap! Flap! The wings are back!

"Woo-hoo!" shouts the boy. He chases after them. "See ya!" he calls over his shoulder. "I need those wings. They're my only hope!"

"**Wait!** I'm Pegasus. Who are you?" I call.

"**Zeus**!" the boy replies. Then he disappears over a hill.

Uh-oh! The sun's going down.

It'll be dark soon. I gallop up the mountain lickety-split. When I arrive at a signpost, I'm huffing and puffing. The sign reads SCHOOL FOR MAGICAL MONSTERS.

Two arrows below the sign point in opposite directions. The one pointing left says CREATURES. The one pointing right says BEASTS.

Um . . . what? Beasts also go to my new school? This is *terrible* news! They're monsters too, of course. But they're mean! They don't like us Creatures. At least that's what I've heard.

To tell the truth, I've never actually met a Beast. Did my family know there would be Beasts here? Maybe not. Or they might not have let me come!

I'm glad I've already made one new friend on Mount Olympus—Zeus! I hope we meet again.

For now I follow the CREATURES arrow and hurry-worry my way to school.

Clip-clop!

2

School for Magical Monsters

Leafy bushes line either side of the path. They're so tall I can't see over them. After turning many corners, I realize something. This path is actually a **maze**.

"A-*maze*-ing!" I say out loud. I

giggle at my joke. *Snort!*

Each time I reach a dead end, there's a sign. NOT THIS WAY, says one. YOU'RE GETTING NOWHERE FAST, says another.

Afterward I have to backtrack to move on. Maybe this is some kind of new-student test. It's a little bit hard, but also fun! Finally I come to the center of the maze. CONGRATULATIONS! YOU MADE IT! says the sign there.

Ahead of me I see a white stone building. It's enormous! It doesn't have walls. Instead, rows of columns hold up its roof. I trot up the stairs and go in.

It's night now. Soft light comes from a lamp, but I don't see anybody. Just a bunch of lumpy blankets on the floor. **"Hello! Anybody home?"** I call.

Creatures leap up from under the blankets. Three of them. Each one looks different from the others, but they all wear caps with a big C on the front and their name below. C for "Creature," I guess.

Scree-ee-ee! Now a fourth Creature swoops toward me from the ceiling. It's part lion and part eagle, with wings, a sharp beak, and claws. It lands in front of me and opens its beak wide.

"Aaagh! **Don't eat me!**" I cry. I stumble backward and almost fall down those stairs I just trotted up.

"Creature or Beast?" the beaky guy squawks. "Which are you?"

"C-C-Creature," I say. "I'm Pegasus. I was invited to go to school here!"

At this news, the guy's beak curls in a smile. *Phew!*

He points to the name on his cap. "I'm **Griffin**." He hops closer and cocks his head at me. "Did you bring any gold?"

"Uh, no. Why?" I ask. "Isn't this school free?"

"Maybe. Maybe not," says Griffin.

"Bull-oney! It's free. He just likes gold is all," another Creature tells me. He's a real bull! One that stands on two feet. The name on his C cap reads **Minotaur**.

Minotaur whips out a bullhorn and roars, **"Listen up, everyone!** We have a new bunkmate—Pegasus!"

A girl nearby covers her ears. "Not so loud!" she says. She looks a lot like me, except more like a *sea*horse because she has a fish-tail. And bubbles float out of her mouth when she talks!

"I'm **Hippocampus**," she tells me. "But call me HC."

"Okay," I say.

Seven eyes are looking at me now. It would be eight, except there's a Creature here with only *one* big eye. Smack-dab in the middle of her forehead! The

name on her cap is **Cyclops**.

Maybe it should be *High*clops, I think. Because she's almost twice as tall as me!

Looking grumpy, Cyclops points to a stack of blankets nearby. "Take one," she tells me. "Then maybe we can all go back to sleep!"

"Sure. Sorry!" I grab a soft black blanket with white stars from the stack. The others **snuggle** under their blankets again.

I'm looking for a place to lie

down when I trip (of course) on a blanket with another lump under it.

"Hey!" A head pops out from under the blanket. It's a human girl! Her black hair is parted in two thick braids. She stares at me in surprise. **"Who are you?"**

I stare back, also surprised. Because what's a human doing in a school for magical monsters? She seems to be wearing a Creature cap, too. It's on backward and turned away from me, so I can't read her name.

"I'm Pegasus," I say. "I'm new here," I add, since she was asleep when I met the others. (Though how she could sleep through that bullhorn is a mystery!) "What's your name?" I ask.

She crawls out from under her blanket. Now I see that she has the body and tail of a lion. And wings and paws. So she's a Creature after all!

She smiles sneakily. "Try to guess it," she says. "Start with a four-letter word that means to turn around in circles. Drop an *H* in the middle of the word. Then add an *X* at the end."

I think hard. "Is the word 'twirl'? No, that has five letters. Wait, I know! 'Spin'! 'Spin' has four letters."

Cyclops leans over. She reaches out one long arm and *spins* the winged-lion girl Creature's cap forward. The girl tries to slap a hand over her name, but it's too late.

I twitch my tail happily. "Aha! Put in an *H*, then add an *X*, and 'spin' turns into your name—**Sphinx**!"

She pouts. "Thanks for messing up my riddle, Cyclops."

"You're welcome," Cyclops replies. Yawning big, she snuggles under her blanket again.

Her yawn makes me yawn too. I lie down under my blanket. Soon

all six of us Creatures are on our way to Snoozeland.

Hmm. Snooze? "**Hey!** I've got a riddle!" I blurt into the quiet.

The other Creatures' heads jerk to look my way.

"What question can you never answer yes to?" I say quickly.

"Tough one," Sphinx says after a few seconds.

"Yeah," HC and Minotaur agree.

"We give up!" Griffin squawks.

Giggling, I tell them my question. "Are you asleep yet?"

The others crack up laughing. Even grumpy Cyclops.

I snuggle in, feeling hopeful and happy. For now, I forget about tomorrow's classes and (eek!) Beasts. Because I've made five more new friends!

3
First Day of Class

"Is this our classroom?" I ask in surprise. It's the next morning, and all six of us Creatures are outside in a round grassy area.

"Yup!" squawks Griffin. "It's called Mighty Meadow."

"Guess why," Sphinx says.

"Because it's *mighty* huge?" I guess.

Sphinx paws her hair away from her eyes and grins. "Nope."

"It's mighty *green*?" I guess next.

"Wrong again," HC butts in. "It's because it's where we learn. Our teacher, **Mr. Chiron**, says learning makes us mighty."

I look around, wondering what we'll learn today. Colorful flags atop tall poles ring the edge of the meadow. There are flowers growing here and there, but they've turned brown. Are they sick?

I start to ask, but my friends have already found places to sit or stand in the grassy meadow. I hurry to do the same. *Oops!* I trip. I tumble into someone and we both fall. I look up to say sorry.

Yikes! I tripped into a Beast! The guy's wearing three beanies on his three heads. Each has a B for "Beast" on it and his name: **Geryon**. With three bodies and four wings, he's even bigger than Cyclops!

"GET. OFF!" Geryon roars. The strong, stinky breath from his three mouths blows my mane back. P-U! It smells like rotten eggs, skunk, and fart all mixed together!

"S-sorry," I stutter. I jump away, hoping the stink won't stick to me.

From out of nowhere a stern voice demands, "Geryon, be nice!" Then, *pop*! Our teacher magically appears at the center of the meadow. He's a **centaur**! Half human and half horse.

Grumbling, Geryon shoots me a mean look and stomps away. But he trips over one of his six big feet. "OOF!" He lands with a thud but jumps up quickly.

Aroooo! A three-headed Beast

dog with lots of sharp teeth howls with laughter. The name on his beanie is **Cerberus**.

I do *not* laugh. Why? Because it feels awful to be laughed at for being clumsy. I should know!

"Please welcome our new student—Pegasus," the teacher says now. He trots over and sets a Creature cap on my head. It has my name on it. Awesome!

"Welcome, Pegasus!" the other students call out. Everyone is looking at me. I hoof the grass, feeling a little shy.

I count six Beasts here in the meadow. With us six Creatures, that makes twelve students total. But soon Mr. Chiron divides us into three groups, with two Creatures and two Beasts in each group.

I'm glad Sphinx is in my group. But not so glad about the two Beasts. The one named **Chimera** has three heads—lion, goat, and dragon. (Gulp!) The other Beast is Geryon. (Double gulp!)

"Listen up, students! Mighty Meadow is in trouble," Mr. Chiron announces. "You've probably noticed that its flowers have turned brown. Today, your task is to help them get healthy again. And to work well together in groups."

If he wanted us to work well together, he shouldn't have put Beasts and Creatures in the same groups, I think. But maybe our teacher hopes this assignment will help us become friends?

Mr. Chiron clicks his boot heels together. Instantly, three red-and-white toadstool tables—one for each group—magically appear. Atop each table are sheets of paper, colored markers, and a bag.

"The assignment for each group is to draw an object to help

save the flowers," Mr. Chiron goes on. "Each group will draw twelve copies of it. Your markers have magic to bring the objects you draw to life, so they can then help the flowers." He smiles, then adds, "Think smart, and be creative. Be your best self, and your special power might find you today!"

Best self? I'm not sure what that means. I've been told that none of the Creatures or Beasts in our class has gotten a power yet. Finding mine would be *sooo* cool! So would brightening the meadow's flowers.

"What're the bags for?" someone asks as we gather around the toadstool tables.

"To collect your objects if they're unable to help," Mr. Chiron says. Then, *pop!* **He disappears!** "I'll *pop* back at the end of class to see how you did!" his voice calls out.

I wonder if he's keeping an eye on us even though we can't see him. Even if he isn't, what could possibly go wrong?

4
Zzzt!

"So what should our objects be?" Sphinx asks Chimera, Geryon, and me right away.

Chimera's goat head shouts, "Maaa-**marshmallows**!"

"How would marshmallows

help the meadow flowers?" Sphinx asks.

"I don't know, but they're easy to draw," Chimera's lion head replies.

"Tasty too!" adds her dragon head.

Geryon raises one of his wings high and yells,

"Ooh! I know! How about seeds instead? To grow new flowers."

"Not a bad idea," I say, backing away from his stinky breath.

Geryon actually smiles at me! It's a scary smile—all Beast smiles seem scary to me—but still.

"Won't it take a while for new flowers to grow, though?" asks Sphinx.

Chimera's heads nod. "You're right."

Just then I get an idea.

"Thunderbolts!"

I suggest.

Sphinx looks alarmed. "Wouldn't those be dangerous?"

"And anyway, how would they help?" asks Geryon. When he isn't shouting, his breath isn't so stinky, I notice.

"We could draw little ones that only tickle the clouds," I say. "With tiny sparks that'll bring rain to perk up the flowers."

Sphinx nods. "None of the other groups will think of bolts, I bet."

"It's a smart, creative idea, like Mr. Chiron wants," adds Chimera. Her praise makes me happy.

Our group gets to work. Each of us draws three thunderbolts for a total of twelve. We put silly faces on them just for fun.

I look over at Geryon's bolts. "You're good at drawing zigzag lines," I tell him.

He sends me another scary smile. "Thanks."

As soon as we finish the thunderbolts, they leap off the paper and become real.

"**Na-na-na-naa-nah!** You can't catch me!" they yell.

The bolts run into one another. *Flash! Crash!* They zip through the air quick as . . . well . . . lightning. But instead of making rain, they make trouble. One bolt lands on my head and does a little dance. *Zzzt!*

"Stop! That tickles!"

Snort-giggling, I shake my head to free it.

Sadly, my idea is a flop. The other two groups' ideas fail too.

One group made watering cans. But instead of watering the flowers, the cans fight. *Clang! Bonk!* "Take that!" they shout, banging their spouts together like swords.

The third group made seeds. Not flower seeds like Geryon's suggestion, though. These seeds are pure gold! Huh? Probably Griffin's idea, since he's in that group.

The gold seeds hop up and down. *Boing! Boing!* They clink against the watering cans and play keep-away from the thunderbolts. Since none of our objects are helping the flowers, we bag them up in disappointment. Griffin takes charge of his group's bag.

He probably hopes Mr. Chiron will let him keep those gold seeds!

My group's bag of bolts is clenched in my teeth when I hear a familiar sound overhead. *Flap! Flap!*

Oh no! Those wacky white wings are back! I guess Zeus, that boy I met on the way to school, hasn't captured them yet.

WHOOSH! They dive toward me. Thinking fast, I swing the bag of thunderbolts to knock them away. Instead, those wings snatch the bag from me and fly off!

"Give that back!" I yell. But the wings only flap faster. Soon they and the bag of bolts are just a faraway speck in the sky.

Great, I think. It's only my first day of class and already I've messed up. Maybe it won't matter that our bolts are gone. It does matter that we all failed the assignment, though. Those poor flowers remain brown. Too bad. I really hoped my thunderbolt idea would work.

5

Beast Bash

My first week at school only gets worse. During races in Mighty Meadow the next day, I step in a hole. I fall flat on my face and come in last.

And when the *popular* Mr.

Chiron lets us play tag in the meadow two days later, I stumble so much I can't catch anyone. I have to stay "it" the whole time. I begin to worry that I might get sent home for being too clumsy!

On Friday, all twelve of us Creatures and Beasts hike up Monster Mountain. On a very bumpy part of the path, I trip over a tree root. *Argh!* I tumble head over hooves downhill.

Luckily, Chimera is below me. *Oof!* I land sitting on her back

behind her lion head. "*Purr*-fect landing!" she jokes. Seems like we sort of became friends while making thunderbolts. She kindly piggybacks me the rest of the way up.

We're learning camping skills today, so we dig a pit atop Monster Mountain. Next, we gather wood and make a fire.

Suddenly the flames leap out of the pit! They swirl around Chimera until they become part of her.

"Hey, everyone! What's happening?" she calls out in surprise. Colorful flames shoot out of her three mouths when she speaks.

"I think you just got your magic power!" I shout. She's the first of any of us—Creature or Beast—to get one.

"Probably because you helped Pegasus up the mountain," Sphinx tells her.

I bet she's right. Being helpful must be part of being our best self!

Chimera smiles at me. Our

friendship just got another boost, I think.

The next morning, she invites me to a party to celebrate her new magic power. "It's at six o'clock at Beast Base," she tells me.

My eyes widen. My Creature friends told me that the only time Creatures and Beasts come together is during class. Otherwise they stick to their own groups. That's just the way it's always been, they said. "But I thought Creatures never set foot, paw, or hoof in Beast Base," I tell Chimera. "Same as how no Beasts enter Creature Camp."

Chimera nods. "Yeah, but it's *my* party. I'll tell the other Beasts I invited you. It'll be fine."

I'm a little scared to go, but I like Chimera. So I say, "Okay, I'll come."

"Guess what?" I say to Sphinx and Griffin later that day. "Chimera invited me to a party at Beast Base tonight. To celebrate her new magic power."

Sphinx's face turns pale. "Party? You mean a Beast Bash?"

"You can't go!" squawks Griffin. "You'll get hurt!"

"Huh? Hurt?" I ask. "What's a Beast Bash?"

"A party where Beasts bash each other with big rocks and sticks!" says Sphinx.

I gulp. "Really?"

"That's what we've heard," she says. "No Creature has actually been to a party at Beast Base before."

"Well, I told Chimera I'm going, so I am." I hope I sound braver than I feel. Griffin and Sphinx trade worried looks. "I'll be okay," I say, hoping I'm right.

With a wave, I head back to camp. Although I've never been to a Beast Bash, I *have* been to birthday parties. So I figure I should bring a gift.

Good thing there's a huge cupboard in our camp building that has everything I need. I will make Chimera a special present for her big day!

When I trot over to Beast Base that night, I'm extra careful. I don't want to trip over my hooves and drop my present! I jump when I hear a weird noise behind me. I look back down the road but don't see anything to worry about. Just my imagination, I guess.

A band is setting up when I arrive. Chimera sees me and waves. **"Yay! You came!"** she calls out.

Beast Base looks a lot like Creature Camp, with a rectangular building open on all sides. Strings of party lights wind around the columns.

Suddenly, Cerberus blocks my

path. "What's in that box? A booby trap?"

"It's a present," I explain quickly. "For Chimera."

"Yeah, right. Go away, *yooou!*" his three dog heads howl. "Creatures can't be trrrusted."

All at once his ears prick up. Looking alarmed, he points to something behind me. "**Ambush!**" he shouts.

Huh? I turn around fast. Behind me stand the other five Creatures! That noise I heard must've been them following me. But why?

As they race toward me, all six Beasts rush to meet them. There's huffing and snorting. Both sides look ready to fight.

"You brought trouble?" Chimera asks me. She sounds hurt.

"No! Sorry. I . . . here, I brought you a gift!" I hand it to her as if that will fix everything.

Flap! Flap! Argh! Those big wings are back. With the bag of thunderbolts they stole!

When everyone stops to look

up, the wings are startled into dropping the bag. All twelve little thunderbolts escape from it! Giggling, they zip from Creature to Creature and Beast to Beast. They zap our heads, backs, and tails. *Zzzt! Zzzt! Zzzt!*

"Ha-ha-ha! **That tickles!**" we call out. We can't stop laughing! We roll on the ground, bumping into one another.

Flap! Flap! The wings come after me now.

"Leave me alone you . . . you ding-a-ling wings!" I yell. I jump up and run, zigzagging between Creatures, Beasts, and bolts to get away. But those wings keep coming.

BOOM! Suddenly a *real, big* thunderbolt lights up the evening sky. Everyone freezes in surprise. Seeing their chance, the white wings swoop toward me. I toss my head and flick my tail, trying to scare them off.

Flap! Flap! Something tickles my back. I'm pulled up and off the ground. Those wings attached themselves to my back! They whoosh me high in the sky.

I'm flying!

6

Magic Wings

"Look! Pegasus just got his magic power!" Minotaur shouts into his bullhorn.

Can he be right? I wonder. If so, I'm the first Creature in our class to get a power! Is that why those wings have been chasing me? Because they wanted to give me the power to fly? But why me? Chimera got her magic power after she rescued me. I haven't helped anyone—yet.

At first it's hard to balance myself up here in the air. When a blast of wind hits me, I spin in circles. I tumble head over hooves. But I soon get the hang of things.

"Woo-hoo! I'm flying!" I shout. When I'm on the ground, I trip

over my hooves. But up in the sky, I'm graceful!

I'm flying high over Mount Olympus when a voice calls, "Pegasus! Over here!"

I look down. In the light of the

moon I see Zeus. He's waving at me from the top of a tree.

"Zeus! **I got my magic power!** Aren't my wings awesome?" I shout.

He waves again, smiling. "Yeah!"

Then I remember that Zeus wanted to capture the wings for himself. "Sorry you didn't catch them," I call.

Suddenly, that big thunderbolt flashes in the sky again. *BOOM!*

Zeus points at it. "It's okay. That big bolt is the magic I'm *really* after. I hoped the wings would help me grab it. But they're meant for *you*, not me."

Did Zeus climb the tree thinking he could reach the big bolt from its top? No way is it tall enough. He needs my help! I swoop toward him. "C'mon! With my magic wings we'll catch that bolt in no time," I tell him. He grins big and leaps onto my back.

We rise into the sky and speed off. When we catch up to the bolt, we circle it. It darts here and there.

BOOM! BOOM! We move closer. *Flap! Flap!* Zeus reaches out. **He grabs it!**

"Gotcha!" he yells. The mighty thunderbolt sizzles and sparks in his hand. But it doesn't try to escape. It seems happy Zeus caught it! Like it knows they belong together.

Zeus raises the bolt high. "With this bolt, I will rule Mount Olympus!" he shouts in a mighty voice. "I will take my proper place as king of the gods."

"Wow!" I say.

He smiles at me. "Thanks for your help, Pegasus. I couldn't have done this without you."

I nod happily. "We make a good team!"

Then it hits me. I must have gotten my magic power because I was meant to use it to help Zeus achieve his **destiny**!

"Now that you have magic too, maybe you can help *me* help some sad flowers?" I say. I explain the plan I've thought of.

"Let's do it!" he agrees.

Together we zoom up to a big gray cloud in the sky above the meadow. Zeus holds his thunderbolt high. Ready... aim... As he tosses it, I trip over the edge of the cloud. Oh no! But luckily my stumble gives his bolt just what it needs—some extra oomph! It hits the cloud dead center.

BOOM! The cloud splits open. *Whoosh!* Rain pours down on the thirsty brown flowers in Mighty Meadow.

Like magic, they turn bright colors. Hooray! We saved them!

The bolt flies back to Zeus's hand. Moments later, I drop him off at the top of Mount Olympus. We wave goodbye.

"See you another day, Pegasus!" he calls to me as I soar away.

The School for Magical Monsters is spread out below me. Beast Base, Creature Camp, and Mighty Meadow. This is where I belong. Where I fit in! Feeling happy, I do some fancy loop the loops. Then I swoop toward the party at Beast Base.

I stumble on the landing. "Oops," I say. I skid to a stop just inches from Chimera.

My classmates don't laugh, however. Instead, they cheer. "You got wings!" Chimera says. "Now *two* of us have magic powers!"

Minotaur blasts the news with his bullhorn, keeping score. "So far it's a magic power tie: Beasts, 1; Creatures, 1!"

"Ye-e-e-es! Isn't it fantastic!" I fold my new wings against my sides. They're part of me now. So is my clumsiness, I guess. And that's okay.

"Sorry we followed you here," Sphinx tells me. "We just wanted to make sure these Beasts didn't bash you."

"Yeah, bashing each other with sticks and stones is not us Creatures' idea of fun!" Griffin squawks.

The Beasts look puzzled. Then they begin to giggle. "We don't bash each other with sticks and stones," says Chimera.

"Right," Geryon says. "We use pillows. **As in pillow fights!**"

My Creature friends and I grin. Because pillow fights are fun!

"Hey! That reminds me of a

riddle," Sphinx says. "Why did Mr. Chiron put sugar under his pillow?"

"Why?" the rest of us ask.

Sphinx laughs. "So he could have *sweet* dreams!"

We all laugh too.

Chimera opens the box I gave her. It's filled with graham crackers, marshmallows, and chocolate. "For making s'mores," I explain. "I know how much you like marshmallows."

"**Yum!**" says Chimera. "I

don't know what s'mores are, but thanks!"

We gather sticks for the marshmallows, and I show everyone how to make s'mores. Using her new power, Chimera breathes fire from all three of her mouths.

Her magical fire breath toasts the marshmallows different colors. Mine turns a sparkly purple, and Sphinx gets a cherry-red one. *Mmm! Tasty!*

The Beasts chow down, then slowly smile their scary smiles. Turns out s'mores are a big hit!

After we eat, the Beast Band plays. They know a lot of great songs. Like "Beast Boogie-Woogie" and "Monster Mountain Mash." Everyone begins to dance. I flap my wings and do a graceful twirl in the air. Then I land on the ground and do a silly, clumsy dance that makes everyone clap.

"Go, Pegasus! You rock!" they call out.

Maybe we Beasts and Creatures are on the path to getting along, I think. Because tonight we're *all* friends. It's so fun! Time for a pillow fight. *Snort!*

Word List

ambush (AM·bush): A surprise attack

centaur (SEN·tohr): A creature who is part man and part horse

clumsy (KLUM·zee): Not graceful

destiny (DEH·stuh·nee): Things that will happen to someone in the future

Magical Monsters (MAJ·ih·kull MON·sturz): Imaginary Creatures and Beasts on Mount Olympus

marshmallow (MAHRSH•mel•oh): A soft, sweet, and chewy candy

maze (MAYZ): A system of paths with many dead ends

Mount Olympus (MOWNT oh•LIHM•pus): Tallest mountain in Greece

mythical (MITH•uh•kull): Imaginary and fantastical

snuggle (SNUG•uhl): Move into a warm and comfortable position

tangled (TAN•guhld): Messy and twisted together

Questions

1. What are three things you like about Pegasus?
2. Pegasus gets teased for being clumsy. Have you ever been teased? How did it make you feel?
3. If you could have a special magic power, what would it be? Why would you choose that power?
4. The Creatures and Beasts in this book don't trust one

another. Why do you think that is? How could they learn to get along better?

5. Mighty Meadow got its name because learning happens there, and learning makes someone mighty. Can you name three ways that learning makes you "mighty"?

Authors' Note

Hi! We are Joan and Suzanne, two friends who have fun writing books together. Our inspiration for the Creatures, Beasts, and other characters in the books comes from **Greek mythology**.

Myths are epic tales of magical beings, bravery, and heroic battles. People made up such tales long ago to try to understand things like thunder.

Pegasus, for example, was

a winged horse who belonged to Zeus, king of the Greek gods. Pegasus helped him by carrying his thunderbolts.

In School for Magical Monsters we bring mythological characters together and let them discover their magic powers.

We hope you have fun reading all of the School for Magical Monsters books!

—*Joan Holub and Suzanne Williams*

From the authors of the bestselling *Goddess Girls* series comes a new set of magical adventures with

Little GODDESS Girls!

Athena & the Magic Land

Persephone & the Giant Flowers

Aphrodite & the Gold Apple

Artemis & the Awesome Animals

Athena & the Island Enchantress

Persephone & the Evil King

Aphrodite & the Magical Box

Artemis & the Wishing Kitten

Athena & the Mermaid's Pearl

Persephone & the Unicorn's Ruby

Aphrodite & the Dragon's Emerald

Artemis & the Dog's Diamond

EBOOK EDITIONS AVAILABLE

ALADDIN | simonandschuster.com/kids

LOOKING FOR YOUR NEXT FAST, FUN READ? BE SURE TO MAKE IT ALADDIN QUIX!

EBOOK EDITIONS AVAILABLE
ALADDIN • SIMONANDSCHUSTER.COM/KIDS